His Lingering Perfume

A raw story of awkward love

Sarah D

ISBN 978-93-5610-507-2

Published in India 2022 by Pencil

A brand of
One Point Six Technologies Pvt. Ltd.
123, Building J2, Shram Seva Premises,
Wadala Truck Terminal, Wadala (E)
Mumbai 400037, Maharashtra, INDIA
E connect@thepencilapp.com
W www.thepencilapp.com

Author biography

You only live once!

With my pen as my sword, I'm going to write my way into the world of romance! I love to write about my experiences since writing is often the best language!

I have recently encountered a revival in my life. You see, I wasn't always the perfect picture of happiness and I feel that God came into my life, and things changed! I now have taken to writing, not to earn my daily bread, but to try and spend time in a wholesome enjoyable way.

I have just graduated from Journalism College, from a reputed university in Goa, where I'm from. While I find that writing is always fun and enjoyable, I like to keep my writing relatable and something I feel that my readers can relate to! I know that some writers expect the world from their writing, but I really want MY readers to enjoy reading about the characters I crafted and try relating to them.

CONTENTS

Acknowledgements

This book is dedicated to my best friends who hold a special place in my heart, and who taught me everything I know about love.

Introduction

Who says awkward people can't be lovers?

They are secret lovers who have known each other for quite a while; She is one of those women who grew up in a rich country yet she hates wearing makeup, which is quite surprising! She is a beautiful woman who was even approached by a modeling scout (since she really is quite the looker, without even trying)

While she could make a completely different impression if she actually tried, but well, that's another story!

He is her secret lover who spices up her life and makes it worth living.

He's far more mature, holding a regular job that he works hard to hold on to, after college hours.

He is such a philosophical guy, with a balanced approach to life! The only immature thing he does is the lengths he goes to maintain his relationship with the object of his affection for her! He even enters her house through a secret route, so they can spend time together and get to know each other better.

In this book, the characters are only called him and her.

The only reason is the fact that it is based on a true story!

How long can they get so close without losing their virginity?

If you are a fan of romance without the additional B.S this book is for you!

Their Love ...

She was indeed a very simple, conservative young woman. The only thing different about her was that she had that "loud thinking" that most go-getters usually had and was really unorthodox in that sense! She hated watching the news, but she was educated in all the right ways! She seemed to know everything that a person, especially a girl needed to get by in today's world.

She didn't like to overgroom (As though grooming was the only thing in life) She hardly ever looked at her reflection in the mirror!

That could be one of the reasons why, even though she actually was very pretty, she never seemed to realize it! It was like she knew... but she didn't really 'see' it.

Not that makeup defined people who people were ever, it did for some people! She had heard that some people liked to define who they were by the way they dressed! She on the other hand, hardly ever applied any make-up on her face! Her friends did! She obviously wasn't like them! She would go everywhere with her hair tied in a simple bun, and she liked it like that for the sake of convenience! She had a lovely, awesome figure, and she liked to exercise! She loved running! She loved waking up every morning to go out for a run in the a.m. sun!

The thing about her was, she was a sporty sort, who liked being just a little bit tomboyish! She was overall a lovely person as well, maybe a little more flawed than others, but a little more real!

She felt that "in this world, people are mostly fakes!" To her, she saw herself as being REAL! She didn't really like the idea of painting her face! The idea of dazzling in silk was not at all beckoning. She preferred to wear simple garments, in spite of which she was a stand-out type! She was the kind of person you noticed when they walked into a room! She was a very attractive young lady!

One morning she tied her hair simply, so it stayed away from her face, the way she usually did it. This was a ritual for her. It was indeed part of who she was. She loved having her hair away from her face, yet to her it was something that was cute even from behind. The whole bun idea was that it was easy to style, the neatest hairstyle, and yet she looked so cool!

She suddenly looked in the mirror and had some rather strange thoughts. She wondered if that woman who she saw in the mirror could be totally different! A completely different individual? A "proper beauty" perhaps?

She corrected herself and said not today! She told herself that she would have worn a hijab and gotten away with it. She reckoned. She grew up and did high school in Dubai. Since she had seen so many Arab women, she had also observed how they were, how some of them liked the idea of the hijab (and some didn't!) But she could relate to the ones that loved their Hijab because she had always been a simple person that could relate to others. She came from a well-to-do family from an affluent neighbourhood and had a sprawling beautiful home.

But she was simple. She was different. You wouldn't even realize that she came from a rich family. She looked like an ordinary person. She loved being average. She was someone who loved the idea of being REAL a little too much!

She stared long and hard at herself. She walked around her dressing table, that day was a different day! She looked in to the mirror and noticed her face.

For once she saw her reflection and liked what she saw! It was indeed a different day, so different, it was strange!

She wondered how suddenly like magic, her features aligned, almost like the planets in the Milky Way. She looked in the mirror a little more closely. She observed for herself that she had nice eyes, a nice nose and nice lips! Since she exercised alot she had a perfect chiselled face and a nice statuesque neck. She also had broad shoulders, slim beautiful arms and a narrow waist! The best part of her was her tiny boyish butt, which she noticed standing sideways in the mirror!

Not one to generally pose a lot in the mirror, even for selfies, she did just on that day! She continued to look-She noticed her slender legs and thighs and her very tiny feet!

She never saw herself that way before but she noticed that she could have looked good in a feminine way as well. As in 'Hot' 'Attractive' and 'Sexy'- she wasn't always in the habit of doing this, but something prompted her to.

She pinched her loose T-shirt at the sides, and saw that she had a very hourglass figure! She was blessed with great proportions, and she thought for a second that she was very umm, luscious.

It was the one day when she looked in the mirror and saw that she was indeed pretty!

She decided to pick up a random lipstick. She picked up what seemed like a pretty pink shade! She was a little tan in color, but the pink suited her skin just fine! She had been watching enough make-up tutorials on YouTube to know that a pink lipstick would suit her even though her skin was dusky! She reminded herself that in today's modern world there were so many dark models she told herself. Why couldn't she be like them?

She pouted in the mirror, made a little made a duckface and started to put the color on her lips! She looked at her face again in the mirror again! She looked at her beautiful pink lips! She really loved her reflection now! She was indeed so happy with it! It seemed to indeed be the thing dreams were made of! The color seemed to beautify her face! A lot! There was such a huge difference! She looked like "a beauteous beast", she felt, whatever that meant!

She really felt she had the makings of a model. That's what a lot of people thought! At least that's what a modeling scout told her when he spotted her when she was out with her friends one day. He worked for Elite Model Management based in her hometown! He had asked her if she would model for a clothing company. She was excited at the prospect, but she didn't reply on time and decided to procrastinate because she REALLY wasn't sure.

She wondered if it were the right thing to do, especially since all the girls were doing it. She turned down the offer since her friends said it was not a decent thing to do! She didn't challenge what they were saying because she felt she was the sporty sort, an adrenaline junkie who didn't care about grooming too much!

She remembered the incident, and looked in the mirror again! She wondered if she was missing an opportunity that could turn her whole life around! She knew she had the looks, but she wondered if she had the motivation. If there was anything that bothered her, it was that one thing. Models had pretty busy lives and hectic schedules, she wondered if she was up for it!

She then took some pretty pink eye shadow that was also on the table! She dipped her finger in it! She had a sister who lived in the Uk, and she would send her little sister loads of make-up! The only problem there was that she never wore it ever! She was so happy being simple.

Whenever she looked in the mirror, she liked her modest look! She felt that she looked like she was a simple girl with simple looks! She knew she had access to make-up, but since she didn't have any friends who liked make-up she wouldn't touch it!

The people she interacted with on a daily basis were her mum, her dad, her sister! They were the only ones she interacted with so she only had them to please! The pandemic was going on, so she wasn't leaving the house all that often! She was starting to feel a bit restricted. She was so used to going out, whenever she felt like, going wherever she felt like!

She applied the light pink eyeshadow to her lids! The eye shadow was a metallic shade, with a strong hint of green. The Greenish eye shadow and pink lipstick didn't go together, but this was something sent by her sis according to her sister's liking. Her sister was an eclectic make-up artist who loved doing both her own makeup and doing make-up on others! She didn't work as a make-up artist, but it was something she did as a hobby, something she did for fun!

Her sister didn't realize that she liked to experiment sometimes with different types of make-up! She was a regular visitor to Sainsbury's. She picked up whatever was on sale! She didn't really think about whether it suited her younger sis or not! She assumed that the younger sis would work it into her style because frankly, there was a good use to everything, and if you mixed colors you could get the right shade! She wanted her sis to multi-task!

Yet she bought a lot of it, it was her gesture of kindness, buying a lot of make-up for her younger sister who she knew was pretty, and deserved it!

Upon applying the make-up, she found that her eyes sparkled! Her light green lids stood out since it was a light color! The color did not compliment her pink lips, but there was a huge difference in how she appeared! She looked so different! She looked so cute!

She looked like one of those good-looking Instagrammers! An Instagram model is usually someone self-made, someone whose make-up was different, and whose selfies were so amazing! The selfies usually generated a lot of likes, and people like that (Instagram models) had a lot of fans!

She didn't seem to realize that the colors didn't match! Yet she loved what she saw in the mirror! Her reflection was cute and beautiful overall!

After getting her hair and make-up on fleek, she decided to wear something a bit different! She walked to her cupboard. She took out a beautiful pink sweater to wear with her jeans. She wore it. She looked in the mirror. She was happy with what she saw! For once she had put in the effort!

She looked so precious! So sweet! You could even use words like "Hottie", "Sexy", "Beautiful", "Attractive" and "Heroine" to describe her!

She then decided to let down her hair. She had long hair. Long hair that was otherwise curly, but she liked to do rebonding. When she did this she looked different. It was a little expensive to do the rebonding, but it changed the way she appeared! She looked in the mirror, her ears were no longer visible.

She decided to look with a look of love. She looked in the mirror again.

Her runaway boyfriend was behind her. He had taken her by surprise! Yes, she had a lover no one knew about! He knew about her simplicity and loved it! He was a simple guy, she was a simple girl. They were a simple bunch in a lonely town. Everyone else was into boozing and partying. These two found solace in each other's company!

He was a nice man to look at too, he himself was so cute.

He had slightly longer wavy hair. His Eyes were brown-green and he had abnormally fair skin. It was indeed nice when people had fair skin. His face was lighter than the rest of him, and his brown hair was his crowning glory falling on his shoulders! He liked to tie his beautiful hair tho,

He held her for a while. Both were staring in the mirror. She noticed his fair skin looked like such a contrast to hers. He had soft hands and he smelled so nice. She really enjoyed being in his arms!

He was as cute as a button! He got into the house through the window. Her parents didn't realize it but this was also her secret route to get out of the house. There was a small room built for guests right outside below her room. There was a way of jumping onto its roof, and then a small hole in the wall where you could put your foot, and slide stealthily down the guest room, and onto the ground floor. She had taught that to him as well. Her parents were strict! But she had a secret life!

He grabbed her from again in a friendly way and started kissing her neck and playing with her boobs. She didn't mind at all. He could see that she had been applying make-up. He found that she was "so much of a hottie in it". He loved her the way she was, he could see the real person behind the seeming confusion- she experienced. The simplicity, the modesty, and all in a town where the folks were different!

He loved that simple sport that she was...he loved her all the same!

They usually loved like a wild racing passion! It was their revenge act against the world. Okay so they didn't drink and they didn't do nightclubs! But they still got the best deal for what it was worth! There was no crime at being in a relationship, like the Lovers in all the Love stories, Romeo and Juliet, Hercules and his Megara, Ariel and Eric...

They were both standing there, kissing, and the moonlight shone in through the window! It was indeed an awesome sight, as much as it was an awesome night! He held her in his arms and she enjoyed the attention! They spent a lot of time like that, touching, kissing, doing what lovers do...

Suddenly they found themselves in her bed, which happened to be opposite the mirror. She took off her pretty pink top, under that she wore a pretty pink bra! Which he saw, and loved. She was weird like that but she did sometimes take care of herself! She was a bit of a beauteous beast like mentioned earlier, taking care of herself and things! Since she knew that she had some potential for beauty which she somehow knew of course.

He knew that too... he didn't mind. It looked for a minute that those were underwire cups. He knew about girls since he did a bit of reading on the internet. He didn't ask why it was a size small. Why there were fat rolls, coming out under them- he probably didn't care, guys were like that, they somehow liked curves.

At that moonlit moment, all he wanted was to make good of his Love. He wanted to hold her. He wanted to make her feel special. She also liked being held. There was a lack of cute guys in the world. One of them was him she felt.

He was good in bed. He was so beautiful, she felt he looked sexier in bed. They were just innocent virgins but they had fun, they didn't cross the line, for fear of being discovered. They also thought that perhaps there was some good about being young and good as well!

Like the tide has seasons and is affected by the forces of Gravity, they too weren't going to stay that way for long! They were after all human right, and they were doing things on and often! So, they say if a thing didn't improve it sort of declined, was that also a law of nature? She wondered...

He was indeed a good guy, a guy with real and honest-to-goodness characteristics, who came from a rich family, someone who did not drink! He was also a bit of a people pleaser with a heart of Gold! She also felt he had nice lips. They were so nice to kiss. Without his shirt on, his chest was so white and his arms were so pink. Before they kissed he would look at her with his big brown eyes, with a cute puppy expression. She knew he was being kind to her in spite of her being a bit weird. His arms roamed around her and he found that she was like an oasis in the desert.

They did everything they wanted... They had such fleeting innocent love. It didn't seem to be a crime! They kissed long, hugged deep and enjoyed making out! It was such a fun thing to experience!

He left because he had to, even he had parents who would get mad if they discovered him.

She went back to being her original self. Her eyeshadow and lipstick had faded from the bouts of passion She got back in bed. He left his shirt behind. She hugged it, and sniffed it, and it had a sweet scent about it. She liked thinking about how he looked so good in it, his beautiful shoulders, with that beautiful brown hair falling on them, and being in his arms. She loved being there, he was a cute lover to have. Indeed so cute.

His perfume lingered on her. It was the only thing she wore all night. She dreamed of him and awoke in the morning thinking she was in his arms. Even though he had already left, his Lingering perfume was still there.

Their Relationship...

She still felt she was just an ordinary girl, even after having such a handsome boyfriend!

She decided to spend hours lying in her bed after he left. She hadn't set her alarm to wake her up since it was the weekend.

she decided that the only way to get up and finally out of bed was to play some lively music.

She loved in particular old music from the 1980s and 90s from when she was growing up.

She was just a teenager back then... she reminisced. Those had to have been the best times of her life. Life as an adult seemed far too complicated. Even the music these days was complicated. Trashy. Jarring. Loud. Always about the video and never about the music. Today's music seemed to lack feelings. She was sure there were many who felt the way she did.

She didn't feel it was worth her time.

She quickly looked for an 80's Vevo playlist on YouTube. She found this great album called *Greatest Hits Of George Micheal.* 'Wake me up before you go' started to play. She used to think George Michael was indeed handsome as a young man.

The peppy song did its magic and helped her get out of bed.

She decided it was time to get things done. She looked at the clock that was on her bedside table. It was already 9:30 a.m.

She was so grateful for the fact that it was the weekend. Sunday was the one day she didn't have to get out of bed. She knew it wasn't exactly a formality. Still, in her pajamas, she sat at the table with her huge bowl of breakfast cereal. She loved the sugar-coated honey fruit loops she was eating.

She started to daydream about the previous night and even though she lived in a swanky rich place she really wished she paid her own bills, and lived her own life!

That way there would be no one to ask or judge. And her lover wouldn't have to come to meet her in secret!

She knew it wasn't going to be easy. But she thought about the life she wanted and wondered for a while.

She decided she was going to have a great Sunday. Suddenly her friend Evie who was a total chatterbox called. Evie loved to talk about EVERYTHING, literally. She was the source of all gossip for her at least.

Evie didn't know when to stop talking. It was sometimes a particularly annoying characteristic, but today she was actually grateful that Evie had called. Sometimes too much time alone was a bit overwhelming. It was just one of the things she could do to kill time on a Sunday other than sleeping of course.

Suddenly Evie started to dole out advice about her boyfriend.

'Oh no, don't you start!' she said to the chatty friend laughing to herself a little.

The talkative friend then chided her saying ' But girl, we have to talk about it!

She asked again "Tell me what happened!"

'Thanks for asking' she replied. 'But I've always been shy. I have never been lucky in love with other guys, I've told you that a dozen times before since you are my best friend!. I never approached any other guy before' she replied.

The talkative girl listened with all her attention 'I really think you are so lucky that you found someone who likes you back. I think you should tell me more, I know you guys are in Love. But I also know you guys meet secretly, and you do things! Evie said again.

She was really in the mood to tell her close sweetheart friend all the juicy details, but she preferred not to, at least not yet. She wondered what she would do without girlfriends! She was such a great person to have in life!

She now thought she would put some clothes into the washing machine that had piled up from the week passed, and go wash some dishes. The place was a mess and Sundays were the best times to take care of it.

She also wondered if she was a little rude to her friend by not talking to her about everything that was on her mind. Her friend really gave good advice too, and she was great company!

Soon she was done with the clothes and the dishes.

She decided to rest. She plopped down onto the sofa. She started to read the Sunday newspaper. On it was the coming week's astrology forecast. She decided to read her horoscope.

She was surprised at what she read!

'Today your lover is going to kiss you in a way you never thought possible!

She was excited after reading this. It made her day!

Again she was in her room, and she was sitting on her bed. She decided she wanted to read an old diary. She had a habit of recording her life in a diary. She had found a diary she had written when she was still in high school, and she really thought it was a good time to read it because it had a lot of interesting reflections from her younger years, which also happened to be the most interesting time of her life.

She flipped to an entry titled "Valentine's Day Birthday party of class 8", and decided to read. Indeed this was a very interesting event! The time she met that cute crush of hers, the one she would never forget!

She skimmed through the lines...as she read the words, the video played in her mind! She felt like her mind had transported her back in time! She had woken up at 8 am on that great day back in time! She had just turned 14! It sure was fun being 14 since it was after all a little better than being 13 that was just a year older than 12...and in 2 years she'd be sweet sixteen! These apparently were her first waking thoughts, at least that's what the diary said!

She kept on reading! She knew that in many great countries of the world, a girl could officially buy her own vehicle when she was 16! She wondered if she too could do this! She wanted to ask her mum, but wait, maybe it was a better idea to wait until she was 16!

She now knew what sort of person she was when she was just 14 years old. She missed those days! It seemed to be so much fun being awkward! She continued reading. At 11 am apparently, she bunked school, and decided to go shopping with friends in a nearby mall. Since it was Valentine's Day, they were all going to have a big splash, and their parent's didn't know!

This was getting interesting. She suddenly felt she needed a glass of water. She had been reading for quite a while. She went to her dresser which had a jug of cold water on it. It happened to have slices of lemon in it. She had gotten the idea from a friend who had impressed on her that adding lemon slices to the water made it tastier and more drinkable, ordinary water was so hard to gulp down!

She was enjoying her tall glass of lemon water when she heard a sound. She turned around and there he was!

She was so happy! She didn't realize it had already gotten late. She was enjoying reading her diary so much! She was so engrossed in it, that she didn't know that he had come. There he was sitting on her bed with a cute smile on his face.

She was a little taken aback. There was something different about him today, she felt. Also he was looking unusually handsome in his jeans and blue t-shirt. He walked towards her, "I missed you" she said, and soon they were kissing. She really felt he had such nice lips that were so sweet to kiss!

He kissed her with a naughty passion and she liked being on the receiving end. She wondered if kissing with an eye open gave one more judgment and control over kissing in general. They were both new to the romance game. However, at that moment time seemed to stand still. All that mattered to her was being in his arms. All that mattered to him, was kissing her and making her feel needed. He knew she was lonely, and he wanted to fill that void. Little did he know how much he was doing it, by being kind to her!

They were kissing for quite a while, and then he wondered if she wanted more. He started to kiss her neck and she rather enjoyed the attention. There they were standing so close, feeling each others breathing, each others heart beating. There they were in the moonlight feeling rather close and like nothing could tear them apart. He could feel that she liked what he was doing, and so he continued.

She started to feel a little weak in the knees since he was kissing her so much. They moved to the couch next to her bed. There they made themselves comfortable and he put her thigh across his knee. That was a really great angle. They then continued having fun. She noticed his cologne. She admired it so much, and interrupted her lover.

"What cologne is that?" She asked.

"Calvin Klein" he replied.

They got busy again. She was really enjoying herself with her lover! He honestly had such beautiful black hair. His beautiful fair skin was nice to touch and really soft and sweet, She took over the kissing now, and started kissing his beautiful jawline. He had a bit of facial hair, but it was exciting to run her fingers through it, and to kiss her lover very impatiently,

He enjoyed it too, and was wondering if being on the couch was still the best place. She wanted him to wait, and he rather reluctantly did. He knew she loved that old hangout spot of theirs. He decided to take over, and started kissing her chest, it was so soft, and it was nice, anyone would have said it was fun to watch them too...

Soon they were doing more than just making out, and he was getting horny. He said to her 'I am so horny right now'

She was like 'Okay but we can't have sex, what if I get pregnant?'

They had a little fun on the couch for a while, and she was satisfied. He left again, with her still asleep. This was their third meeting in her room, given that they had met only twice before that! She woke up in the morning and again he had left his shirt behind. She liked sniffing it when he wasn't there. She felt so grateful that he was her secret admirer. He also was a kind and understanding lover, it seemed.

After a while she got out her laptop, and started to try her hand at writing a lifestyle blog! It was a Monday, so it seemed like the perfect day to look for jobs online, so she could earn a little money using her writing, since she felt she had it in her to be a writer. She decided to do her homework before she started working on her blog. She decided that Wordbase was a good platform to work with and started to write a blog that catered to plus size women who were unhappy about their weight. She felt she had it in her to motivate people; she felt that her blog could go places!

She worked on the blog for a while. On the other side of town, He (her lover) was having difficulties.

He had'nt gotten a wink of sleep since his foray into Jenna's house. Jenna was of course his muse, his secret lover, his long-time friend and they had only recently changed over from friends into lovers. He was tired but he missed her. He also couldn't stop thinking about the time when he had mentioned that he was horny, and that she had said 'nothing doing' but he stuck around to satisfy her as if they were really doing the real thing.

He missed his funny awkward girlfriend. He enjoyed every minute that he spent with her but he also wondered how long they would be virgins as things were getting hot and heavy between them. She seemed to be a nice girl, he could understand where she was coming from, what she meant by withholding the main event. She obviously felt she was a little unprepared, and also afraid of a pregnancy scare!

He, very unlike Her, was working a part-time job as a call center executive after college hours! He really was articulate like that! He not only managed to be an A grade student which was surprising as it was for a boy, but he also did work after college to supplement his income. He really was a responsible young man, trying to do things on his own, not depending too much on his folks, or taking it easy because he still was after all in college. He wasn't the type to date, and spend too much time with friends. He knew college wasn't going to last forever and that one day he would have to be a full-fledged adult like his older brother.

He came from a family of well-educated and scholarly types. He knew he could never be like his elder brother! His older brother was now an established lawyer who got through Harvard. Ben had inherited that intelligence from his brother and father. He however had gotten the carefree and lenient attitude from his mother.

He was a wonderful young man, but much like her, they were outcasts in their little town. All the rich kids from their neighborhood were into gambling, drinking, and bad company. However who knew how they were different and found each other in the midst of all the noise, the din happening all around! It was like a higher force perhaps the universe, had led them to where they were. In each other's company to learn from each other, to fight against the world and its ways as it were.

Back at her place, it had been a while since she had turned down the offer to pour out her heart to her friend, who was begging and pleading almost for her to tell about what had transpired between her and her soul-friend. She had been through a lot in the little town, for turning down opportunities to be wild and popular like the other rich girls her age. More than anything she wanted to share with her friend but she felt that perhaps she shouldn't? After all, it was private? She knew girls loved to dish out juicy details, but the fact was she was being protective of their relationship. She also knew that her friend was a bit of a chatterbox who couldn't keep things to herself.

Yet she wondered if getting the advice of a buddy would help to get some insight as to what the neighboring folks were thinking. She knew that rebelling against everyone 'to do what she thought was right' was not the right way to go about it. Her friend was always a chatterbox but there was lots to understand about the rest of the world and what they thought. Jenna had lived a protected and sheltered life ever since she was little. However she knew that to spread her wings she had a lot to learn.

She loved him and perhaps dreamed of getting her own place too, but she had dreams. She always wanted to get a small-time job in a quiet place somewhere far from all the rich revelers from where she hailed. They probably all started small too. Depending on her parent's wealth was not something she necessarily thought was best for her. Yet she knew that rebelling against her parents and walking out was not a wise thing to do, as the world was a big bad place with traps and snares at every turn.

Funny enough She had always been "a good little girl" as it were, and as they say, she was growing up tenderly yet sweetly and preciously even in the sight of her parents. She kept her parents happy, and they were happy that their child did not do what the others did, even when presented with the opportunity to do so. It was not like she did not attend any parties. She did. But she chose not to drink, behave weirdly or dress immodestly. She in fact came out of those loud and noisy parties after some well-thought-of 'social networking', a brainchild of her own thinking, making like-minded friends, and learning a thing or two about life and how to deal with it.

All she could think about, for now, was the awesome time she would spend with Ben when she got out into her own little place. She was a shrewd girl like that, given half a chance, not easily swayed by trends, rumors, and gossip as these things had not fazed her ever since she was a young child. Yet at the same time she was wondering if she was missing something by not confiding in her friend, as she after all was a girl, and who better to get advice about relationships from, than from another woman?

She decided to call up her sister who lived in the Uk instead. She made up her mind that she would avoid certain topics rather than resist them. In that way she could get an honest opinion and some perspective as well as share what she felt about him, a sweet guy, but a guy after all! Who better than her older sister to ask about her boyfriend to decide how to break the news to her parents, and how to take the next best steps?

She decided to pick up her phone and call her up! Her elder sister was a good girl who was also a good friend and confidant. She was a lot older than her, so she probably knew better. Her older sister was plain to look at, but her intelligence and mature attitude to life made her a really good person to confide in.

She dialed her number and immediately the older sister picked up the phone.

"Hi sis, it's me" she said

'Hi, what's up?"

" There's something I have not been telling my parents..."

"Okay, this sounds deep! Does this involve a boy, by any chance?"

"Good guess! I know he sounds nice...but I've been meeting him, you know Him, the basketball star, the one who's also really good at studies..."

"I suppose you two have every right to hang out, as long as you do not go too far? You are still young and you haven't finished with college...you understand what I mean by going too far now, don't you?"

"Yes, thanks. If I need to talk, I hope I can confide in you"

"We are friends, right? of course, yes"

"Thanks!"

Saying that she put down the phone, and continued to think about her plans for the rest of the evening.

Their Kiss...

So that night she sat on her bed, looking out the window.

She was waiting for him to arrive, that sought-after secret lover of hers, sought-after in her eyes at least, the man, the beautiful man that no heartthrob could overthrow, no celebrity could replace...For her this guy had a special place, he was a different sort altogether...

She thought about all that had happened between them. She thought about her past. She thought about the times when she as a young child took a step back and thought about things before she did them. She thought about the times when there were many achievements but none as sweet as this one person.

She hardly noticed that she was thinking so deep when she felt an arm on her shoulder. She was a bit taken aback, but then the arm circled her waist and pulled her close for a kiss.

What a deep melting kiss, and the moonlight shone on him now, and he sat there on the bed with her looking at her face and smiling. He then held her hand.

She looked at the precious sight he was. How cute he was looking in that pale blue shirt and dark blue jeans. How cute their legs looked sitting side by side. She could feel some romantic jostling energy between them, She looked at his face again. It was so white and light since he was a fair guy. His big deep black eyes. So cute.

He looked at her, there was definitely some chemistry happening there.

They were kissing again as most lovers do... He started kissing her on her lower lip, and biting it ever so slightly, nibbling on her ears and kissing her chin, weren't they having fun.

Suddenly they were lying down, he kissed her neck very sweetly, kissing down its nape and biting on her collar bones very gently.

Her tummy felt strange, they were close to having sex, but she felt butterflies. Or was it some weird kind of aching sensation, possibly a need to fill a void of some sort.

So she interrupts him and says "You know, at this moment, I wish I were a mermaid"

"What....why?" he said. He knew she was a funny girl, so he took it as a sweet joke and laughed to himself.

"They can't have sex, but they are so hot and frisky all the time" she replied.

"I wish you were a mermaid," he said.

"I can be" she said.

"Okay," he said.

She had watched a dozen movies where the heroine got what she wanted. She wasn't sure if she wanted to be that sort of heroine. She wanted to make her friend here feel special and wanted. After all, he would be leaving in some time.

He held her hand again, "you know there is nothing cuter than you, and for me, you are a dream come true?"

He leaned in again and kissed her neck several times, weren't those some very hungry kisses. She really liked being at the center of the attention. she asked him if he wanted to take off his shirt. He did.

She saw that he wasn't perfect like a model was, but to her he was more than perfect. There was nothing better than having a shirtless man that looked like that in her bed! She cupped his face in her hands and kissed him again. They both closed their eyes. The moon was shining even brighter than it normally did.

She did the same things he did, she kissed his neck and kissed his collarbones and then knelt down on the bed and played with his hair.

He was now lying down and she massaged his shoulders and he felt good, I can see the moon from the window she said. See how its staring at us!

She continued kissing his chest and his tummy and ignored the situation that needed attention in the middle. Then she kissed his thighs and his toes. Nice feet and she made him feel good kissing them as well.

"I think you would make a great mermaid...because we didn't have sex but you still managed to make me feel good"

"I didn't know it was possible for a guy and a girl to get that close and not wind up having sex?"

They finally did not have sex, but yes, she did manage to keep his horny feelings at bay. He was really horny but her gentle approach saved the day, didn't it. She wanted to make her lover feel good, she did. Yet she was too young and possibly too immature to have a baby.

The mysterious lover was satisfied and slipped down the stairwell again. Off he went, into the deep and into the dark, back to his home. He too had parents who would be angry if they found out that their son wasn't home. They were the virgins in the town. But they didn't lack anything like the other people who supposedly had it all going for them.

She was so pleased with herself. She went to the bed to sleep, after all it was late. Again he had left his blue shirt behind. She cuddled with it and it was so filled with the scent of his idyllic cologne..she slept really well that night.

Several years later...

As you can guess these two never got married...

This is an excerpt from her diary

"Years later we met again. I now owned a little cafe in a small town. Those blue eyes. We met again. 'Hi,' he said. 'Hi, is it you?' I replied. It was closing time. He asked me if I was still single. I replied to him that after him there had been no other guy. He then told me that there was no other woman in his life either.

We started kissing. I got lost in those eyes that day. I was so grateful that he came. His kisses were so sweet and so full of passion. After he kissed me I wasn't satisfied. I wanted more. Being on the shorter side I couldn't get enough of the big tall babe that was kissing me. I liked that he was so tall and he managed to overpower me and take control of me with just one kiss.

Soon we were doing it. Again after all these years. I couldn't get enough. He could read my mind. The eyes, the smoldering eyes. There was nothing better.

We were watching the sunrise together. I asked him 'back in college what did you see in an introvert like me?' 'I saw everything- the sun, the moon, and the stars. I saw you exactly the way you are.'

'Why did you fall for the captain of the basketball team?' he asked.

'I loved you because there has never been another mirror to my soul like you.' Cuddling, watching the sunrise together was an experience like no other.

I know I had these dreams of getting married, but we parted ways again. He was the best thing that ever happened to me. I loved him, he loved me right back! No other guy saw what he saw in the Introvert that is me. Life was a breeze as long as I knew him, and I swear I live a little larger because of this beautiful human.

He isn't in my life right now. I'm 70 years old today. I live alone. I pray that I will go to the next world. But to me,

He is a man who will always be 'the most beautiful a man can ever be. I still remember that lingering perfume, of that hottie I once knew and the memory keeps me fit and wanting to be happy and harmonizing with everyone I meet and everything I come into contact with'